Princess Daisy

Kirstin Glover

To order additional copies of this book, contact:
Xlibris
UK TFN: 0800 0148620 (Toll Free inside the UK)
UK Local: 02036 956328 (+44 20 3695 6328 from out-
side the UK)
www.xlibrispublishing.co.uk
Orders@ Xlibrispublishing.co.uk

ISBN: Softcover   978-1-6641-1202-5
        EBook   978-1-6641-1203-2

Library of Congress Control Number: 2020913610

Print information available on the last page

Rev. date: 07/28/2020

Dedication

I dedicate this book to my beautiful Daisy Flower.

Daisy Grace said
to Bella Bee,

'Come with me.

A princess I
will be.'

1

'Over the bridge

To a troll named Jessica Cress,

She can sew the perfect princess dress.'

'Into the cave

To meet a dragon called Faye Brown,

She can make the finest crowns in town.'

'Through the woods

To see Eleanor Snooze,

A unicorn who will have sparkly shoes.'

'Across the meadow

To find the gnome Gregory Bond.

He will give me a magic wand.'

9

'I look in the mirror,

And what do I see?

A princess staring back at me.'

Fairy's House

'Now that I'm a princess,

There's a lot I need to know.

So off to Annabelle, the wise old fairy, we go.'

'A princess needs
to curtsy and
smile.

Manners are
important too,

So don't forget
to say please and
thank you.'

15

'I can see the castle

Sparkling in the sun.

It's time to go home, now that we've had our fun.'

'Today has been long and magical.

Thanks, Bella Bee,

For coming on this adventure with me.'

Acknowledgements

I would like to thank my mum, Shirley, my dad, Robert, my husband, Matt, and my brother-in-law, Aaron, for their support throughout this process.

Lightning Source UK Ltd.
Milton Keynes UK
UKHW050416110820
368025UK00002B/83